My Cowboy Crush

Cowboys of Sunnydale, Volume 0.5

Allie Bock

Published by Allie Bock, 2020.

Table of Contents

Chapter 1 1
Chapter 2 7
Chapter 3 12
Chapter 4 20
Chapter 5 34
Chapter 6 46
Epilogue 57
Falling for My Cowboy Chapter 1 59
Author's note 65
Acknowledgements 66

Copyright

Copyright © 2020 by Allie Bock
All rights reserved. No part of this publication may be reproduced, stored, or transmitted in any form or by any means, electronic, mechanical, photocopying, recording, scanning, or otherwise without written permission from the publisher. It is illegal to copy this book, post it to a website, or distribute it by any other means without permission.
This novel is entirely a work of fiction. The names, characters, and incidents portrayed in it are the work of the author's imagination. Any resemblance to actual persons, living or dead, events or localities is entirely coincidental.
Cover Design by Tubboat Design
First edition

Dedication

To Zack. I know reading romance isn't your thing, but thank you for reading my stories and being a great little brother.

More Books by Allie Bock

<u>Cowboys of Sunnydale Series:</u>
My Cowboy Crush
Falling for My Cowboy
Second Chance with My Bull Rider
My Unexpected Hero
My Cowboy of Convenience

Find out more about Allie's books at:
<u>Alliebock.com</u>[1]
<u>Alliebock.substack.com</u>[2]

---

1. https://alliebock.com

2. https://alliebock.substack.com

Chapter 1

Katie

I strode up the stone pathway to the white doors of the park pavilion. Nerves shook my body causing my palms to be clammy, my heart pounded, and my body to sweat more than normal. *Breathe, Katie. You've got this.* I closed my eyes for a second to steel my nerves. Then, I pushed open the doors with a loud screech. Swarms of women scurried around the large open room. No one noticed me as I took another step inside. A large breath escaped as I scanned the room for the one person I was looking for.

"Katie, you finally made it!" The bride-to-be rushed at me from the center of the room.

Everyone stopped what they were doing to watch us. My anxiety skyrocketed, making my chest hurt. I rubbed at my sternum as I took in another breath. They paused for a moment before resuming their decorating.

"Um, I just got here."

The bride-to-be, Annie, wrapped me into a big hug and bounced up and down.

"I'm getting married!" She screeched.

I winced at the pitch, but I couldn't help smiling at the other woman. Her shiny black hair bounced around her shoulders. It contrasted nicely with her ivory lace dress and faded cowboy boots.

"I'm just so glad you are here," she whispered in my ear, "Come on."

She took my hand and led me to the far corner. She opened a small door and shoved me into a dark closet. The door shut softly behind her with a click. The dust tickled my nose as the moldy smell suffocated me.

"What are we doing in here?" A sneeze erupted from my nose.

I covered my mouth and nose with my hand. My eyes adjusted to the darkness. Cobwebs suspended in the corners. A couple of discarded folding chairs leaned against the back wall. A large yellow spider dropped from the ceiling and hung inches above her head as she leaned close to me.

"I need your help." Her blue eyes grew wide as they searched my face.

"OK." *Where is she going with this? Is that spider going to drop on to her head?*

"Katie, pay attention."

"Sorry, there's a big spider up there."

"Don't worry about the spider. I need your help."

"You've said that."

"My wedding photographer is in the hospital."

"Oh no." I gasped, inhaling a breath of dust. Coughing. "Is everything alright?"

"Her baby was born a preemie. They are both still in the hospital. I know that this is a lot to ask, but you're the only one that can help me." Tears glistened in the corner of her eyes. "Can you, please, take pictures of the wedding? For me?"

I backed up until my back hit the wall. A shower of dust fell onto my shoulders. The large yellow spider scuttled back up her silk to hide in the rafters.

"Um, doesn't she have a backup?" I coughed and sputtered in the dust.

"It was supposed to be her partner but she got thrown from a horse and broke a leg. I need you to do it."

I glanced around but there was no way out. My palms started to sweat, again.

"But I only do landscape and nature photography." Panic rose in my chest.

"Please." She clasped my hands in hers.

"But photographing people is hard. They don't listen to me." My hands shook. "The lighting has to be perfect. Everyone needs to be looking at the camera." My thoughts jumped ahead and I got lost in them for a minute. "Plus, it's a wedding. I've never done a wedding before!"

"But you do such beautiful work. How hard would it be to add people to your landscapes?"

How hard indeed? "People" My voice sounded weak to my ears. My mind trudged like it was stuck in fudge. "It's not really in my wheelhouse. Or even within a hundred miles."

"Please, say you'll do it for me? It's my wedding, I need this to be perfect."

I nodded. *That didn't make me feel any better. But this was a big deal for Annie. And she had always been a big supporter of my work.*

"I want this to go well. If you do it, you'll be saving the day." She pleaded.

My heart sunk at her words. Annie was always good at getting me to do things for her. She knew what buttons to push to get me to cave. And she did need help.

"Fine, I'll do it."

She squealed and gave me another hug before opening the closet door.

"Perfect! Here is a list of pictures I want to be done." She thrust a large binder into my hands. "See what you can do. Here's the itinerary for the wedding. And I'll get you an assistant." She bustled away.

An assistant? I sat down on a nearby bench as my head swam. My relaxing weekend away to see my old babysitter get married just turned into the stuff of my nightmares.

Levi

I slapped the dust from my cowboy hat before shoving it on my head. I loved my sister, but the whole wedding nonsense drove me crazy. I'd rather be branding two hundred calves than delivering Annie's wayward balloons. But here I was. My fist grabbed a hunk of ribbon and tugged the fifty white and ivory balloons. They fought for freedom, blocking my view as I stumbled my way into the pavilion. I fumbled for the doorknob until the door opened and I stepped into the large room. A couple of balloons stuck to the door frame, stopping my forward progress. I turned to pull them into the room. With a loud squeak, they released from the door frame. I stumbled backward, my arms flailed, and balloons floated to the ceiling. With a thud and a soft cry, someone broke my momentum. We went down in a pile of arms and legs.

"Levi, are you OK?"

Annie bent over me as she extracted the woman underneath me. She was curvy with bouncy blonde hair. She straightened her skirt before looking at me. Her blue eyes widened when our gazes met. The breath caught in my throat as recognition dawned on me.

"You remember Katie Kisment?" Annie flung an arm over the girl's shoulders.

"Of course." I swept my cowboy hat from my head as my heart thundered in my chest. "It's good to see you."

A pretty blush colored her cheeks. *Boy, has she grown up.* I haven't seen her for five years when she went off to college. Back then, she was a shy teenager who'd barely say hi to me. She dyed her pretty blonde hair black and wore baggy black clothes. She didn't smile much and hid behind chunky black glasses. I preferred her current natural blonde and blue glasses. She looked lovely and my body responded to her. I could stare into her blue eyes forever.

"Earth to Levi." Annie waved her hand in front of my face.

"Yup." I drew my gaze from the stunning beauty next to her and collected the balloons I could reach.

"Katie needs an assistant for the wedding. And I need you to help her."

I froze in mid-reach. I loved my sister but I was trying to stay out of the wedding. I just wanted to shine my boots and walk my mother down the aisle.

"What?" I stuttered.

"She's going to be my photographer since my original one is in the hospital. She needs help and you're going to help her." She poked me in the chest, hard. She spun on her heel and stalked off to torment someone else.

I caught the last balloon before turning to Katie. Her eyes were wide and her mouth opened into a little O. I smiled at her as she wrung her hands together.

"I don't know anything about being a photographer's assistant."

"That's fine." A smile tugged at her lips. "I've never done a wedding." She stage whispered, causing me to laugh.

"That makes two of us. I'll take these over to my mom." I motioned to the grey-haired woman by the archway. "Then, I am at your beck and call." I winked at her as I walked past.

My head spun as I crossed the room. I had to spend the next thirty-six hours being with the one girl I've crushed on. The one girl that was off-limits, because I worked for her family. There were three rules to working on the Kisment ranch. No fighting, no drugs, and no dating their only daughter. It was shaping up to be a long wedding. I had to live the next several hours without losing my heart or my job.

Chapter 2

Katie

I clutched the binder and iternary to my chest. My heart pounded so hard I thought others could hear it. *Levi was going to help me take pictures. He was going to help me take pictures of people, at a wedding.*

I didn't know which one was more anxiety-producing. The handsome cowboy with his shaggy black hair and dark grey eyes, taking pictures of people, or hoping that everything turned out great because these were once in a lifetime wedding photos. I searched in my pocket for a Tums. No luck. Levi walked to the archway where his mother was attaching balloons to it. His jeans looked good on his long legs. What was I thinking? *Get it together, Katie.* He was not my type. He'd never noticed me before, even when I had a huge crush on him in high school. Those were the days. My tongue swelled in my mouth and my throat closed up whenever he glanced my way. Shaking my head to clear my thoughts, I headed outside to my truck. The noon sun beat down on the asphalt and heat rose from the surface. It was going to be a scorcher this weekend. It was always hot in south Texas on the Fourth of July.

"I should've worn shoes," I muttered to myself as my flip flops slapped the pavement.

The heat started to burn the bottom of my feet. Finally, I reached my beat-up old truck. The paint was peeling from the doors and an old dent stood out on the tailgate. I pulled out my camera and checked the lens. Everything was in my bag. Annie was lucky I traveled with my camera at all times. The perfect picture could happen at any time. I slung the nylon strap over my head and opened the binder on the hood of my truck. There were pictures of people posing by trees, in long grass, by a waterfall, being backlit, and close-ups.

"She doesn't do anything halfway, does she?"

"No, she doesn't." The low timbre of his voice jolted me from my thoughts.

"Don't sneak up on a girl." My hand flew to my chest to contain my galloping heart.

"It's impossible to sneak wearing spurs." He set one booted foot on the tire of my truck and leaned toward the binder. The spur in question glinted in the sunlight. "She has a lot of ideas." He turned the page. "Are you going to get all of these?"

I shrugged. "I've to check out the park first and see what would work."

"Ma'am, I am at your service." He bowed low, sweeping his hat from his head.

He winked as he straightened to his full height. He was a whole head taller than me. Most men were as I was barely five foot three. The grey in his eyes was the color of storm clouds on a winter day. He gently touched my shoulder, jerking me back to reality.

"Katie, are you ok?"

"Yep, never better." I snapped the binder shut, grabbed my backpack from the passenger seat, and placed the binder in it. "Let's get started, cowboy."

I marched off to the grove of trees beside the pavilion. Levi's spurs jingled with each step he took as he followed behind me. I sighed. It was going to be a long weekend.

A few hundred yards away from the pavilion was a small stand of oak trees. Their trunks twisted to the sun while pale green lichen grew on their bark. These weren't the stately oaks of the east, but their wiry, scrappy cousins. They fought against drought, extreme heat, and pests. The trees intertwined in a complicated dance with their branches reaching out over an open space. I marked off the area and framed it out in my mind. I took a couple of practice shots, but without people, it would be hard to tell.

"Levi," I turned to where he stood, leaning against a tree. "Can you stand between the trees? I need to be able to gauge the lighting."

His brow furrowed at my request.

"The wedding will be in just over 24 hours from now. The light will be similar. Please."

He slowly made his way to the center of the trees and shoved his hands in his pockets. I snapped a picture. I groaned when I looked at it on the screen. It was awful.

"No, stand like this." I placed my hands on his shoulders to turn his body.

Electricity ran up my arms. A half-smile pulled at his lips as he watched me. A blush spread up my neck as I turned him this way and that.

"Now, stay like that."

"Yes, ma'am." A grin cocked on his lips.

I shook my head as I marched back to my spot and took some more pictures. The butterflies in my stomach danced. *Keep your focus, Katie.* I moved from side to side and changed the height of my shot. He flexed his biceps, placed one foot on an imaginary rock, fanned himself with his hat. His antics helped me to relax as I worked on getting the best exposures. I jotted down which ones worked well all the while trying to hide the growing amusement as he clowned around. He leaned against a tree and used his cowboy hat to cover his face, pretending to fall asleep. Soft snore came from him. I crouched down to get a different angle. A flash of red caught my eye.

"Let's go over there." I pointed to a rose-covered archway.

I strode down the path and around a bend. The archway stood at the end of the path. The scent of roses filled the air. A small bench sat under the arch. A bubbling of water drew my attention to a quaint water fountain. It was the centerpiece of this quiet sanctuary in the park.

"This is perfect." I blew out a breath.

I brought my camera up to look at it through the lens. I needed to back up to get enough of the arch. I bumped into a solid mass. His spicy scent washed over me as his hand grasped my elbow to steady me. My breath caught in my throat.

He leaned down and whispered in my ear. "Where do you want me?"

A shiver ran down my body as my stomach twisted into a knot. I twisted around to meet his eyes. He smiled down at me. The skin wrinkled at the corners of his eyes. His hat shielded his face.

"Under the arch." I stepped away from his touch and pointed to the bench. "Sit on the bench, please."

He settled on the bench, resting his boot heels on the seat. He winked at me before closing his eyes and leaning back on the seat. The angle was not right. It distorted the picture. I needed to get up higher. I stepped up on the edge of the fountain. The next few shots of the cowboy in the archway were almost perfection. My anxiety over the wedding gradually dissipated as I took another picture. As long as the handsome cowboy kept his distance, my heart might stay whole.

Levi

I closed my eyes to enjoy the sunshine as she capered about taking pictures of me under the arch. The smell of roses overwhelmed my senses. I brought my hat over my eyes as I pretended to be anywhere else but here. Somewhere I didn't have to drag my gaze from the beautiful woman engrossed in her pictures. Her nose wrinkled as she concentrated, her blouse gapped when she squatted down, and her jeans hugged her curves nicely. It was getting hard not to notice her, especially when we touched and it felt like my whole body was magnetized to hers. She mumbled to herself, breaking the silence. I cracked one eye open to watch her as she balanced on the edge of the fountain. If she fell in, it would make it hard to look away.

"Levi, wake up. I'm done here. Let's go over there." She hopped off the stones and walked to a large open grassy area

I groaned as I slowly got up and stretched. My watch read a little after 1:00 PM.

"Yes, ma'am," I called after her.

She waved her hand in the air and kept going. Man, she looked good, walking away. Curves in all the right places. I wondered if she has a boyfriend wherever she's living. A jolt of jealousy shot through me. Why did it matter to me if she had someone? But it did matter. I jogged after her. My spurs jiggling with every step.

Chapter 3

Levi

"Well, I think that's it for the park shots." She consulted the binder and the notebook that she was carrying. "Onto the wedding chapel, do you know where that is?"

"Yep, I sure do."

I made my way to Katie. I grasped her small hand in mine and led her across the green grass of the meadow to the little white chapel hidden behind some evergreen trees. Her hand was warm and soft in mine. They were stained a little bit at the tips of the fingers. I was about to rub my thumb over hers when a gasp escaped her lips.

"Oh, it's so romantic." Her eyes lit up and she dropped my hand like a hot potato.

Her jean-clad legs carried her through the front door. They hugged her perfect curves as if they were painted on. My hand ran through my hair before I followed her. The little chapel had large stained-glass windows with designs of flowers and animals that let the light streak across the floor. White folding chairs had been placed in rows leading up to the archway filled with balloons. I leaned against the wall as she took the area in.

"I don't get it. Where is Annie going to get ready before the wedding?"

"At the pavilion. She and her girls are going to get dressed, and, I guess, take pre-wedding photos. Then, a carriage will take them up to the chapel."

"How romantic." She pulled up her very large camera from around her and took some pictures. "Lightning in here is odd." She scrunched up her nose. "I'm not exactly sure, but I think I'll have to get you to set up some lights in the corners for the shots of the ceremony."

I grunted in response. I was mesmerized by the concentration on her face.

"I want you to go to the front and stand there like you are getting married yourself."

She was looking through the viewfinder in her camera and didn't see me smirk at her. My boot heels clicked along the wooden floor as I made my way up to the archway of ivory and white balloons. I thought about if I'd ever had the desire to get married. I closed my eyes for a moment. There stood Katie in my dreams with a white dress. Her long curly hair pulled up into some sort of fancy updo. She walked down the aisle on the arm of her daddy, carrying a large bouquet of whitish flowers. Wow, where did that come from? I hadn't seen her in several years, and only spent the last couple of hours with her. I mentally shook myself and opened my eyes. Katie was busy snapping shots of the room from the middle of the aisle, over in the corner, and another where the couple would be standing. She was so engrossed with her photography that she seemed not even to know that I exist. It allowed me to check her out freely. Her golden hair was pulled back into a bouncy ponytail. A white blouse with blue flowers gapped when she crouched down. She grew into a beautiful woman. When did that happen?

Katie glanced around the inside of the building until her gaze settled on a platform raised in the air. There was a rickety old ladder that led up to the platform.

"I need to get up there. I think I can get some absolutely fabulous pictures from there." She waved her hand at it before settling her camera against her chest.

"I'm not sure that is a safe idea." I scratched my head.

I studied the platform. It probably hadn't been used in years. Sunlight showed through the gaps in the boards where they had rotted away. Katie was already on her way up the ladder. She climbed up hand over hand, grasping each wooden rung of the ladder. I rushed to her side from across the room just as she put her foot on the next stop. A loud crack sounded throughout the room. She let out a cry as she fell back toward the floor. My arms reached out and caught her. She felt warm and soft in my arms as I held her close to my body. My heart thundered in my chest. Her yellow locks fell across my shoulder. Her big blue eyes widened as she searched my face. My heart pounded as my chest constricted. My mind blanked. Her lips parted with a little gasp. I leaned in close. My lips closed the distance to her lips, as the door swung open.

"What are two doing?" Annie stood in the doorway with her hands on her hips.

Annie's skirt swung against her legs. She lifted an eyebrow as a smile fought for purchase on her face. She broke the spell over Katie and me. I froze for a minute before I set her feet back on the floor.

"We're going over the chapel, just like you wanted." My voice sounded odd to my ears as my throat was thick.

"Sure, you were," Annie smirked. "Looked like more than that."

Katie backed into the shadows where she straightened her blouse. She continued to stare at her feet as a bright flush colored her cheeks. She tucked a strand of hair behind her ear before pulling her shoulders back. Boy, did she look beautiful. Annie threw looks between the two of us.

"So, nothing at all is going on."

"That's right," Katie said. "I was just taking pictures to get ready for your wedding." She fiddled with the strap of her camera. She seemed to shrink into herself.

"Well, it's almost time for the rehearsal dinner. I need to get ready." Annie spun on her heel and strode out the door.

"I didn't..." I ran my fingers through my hair.

Katie interrupted me. "Never mind, it's all right." She hurried out the door after Annie.

Katie

That was a close one. My lips were inches away from his. The high schooler inside of me was about to scream with joy; while, the grown woman part of me was shaking in her shoes. *Breath, Katie. Just like your counselor said.* I murmured to myself as I made my way to my truck. My anxiety was skyrocketing. It felt like a basketball was thumping around in my chest. What was I thinking? Almost kissing Levi. He was known to be a ladies' man. My brother, Kaleb, told me he had a new girl every weekend. That would be the last thing I needed would be to fall for him. I had to protect my heart better.

I reached my truck and looked at the itinerary for the wedding as I sat in the front seat. The wedding walk through and rehearsal dinner didn't start for another two hours. That's just enough time to drive home to see my mom.

It had been a long five years since I drove up the long winding driveway to my family's ranch. The ranch horses were in the field to my left; they frolicked around after a long day of work. A white Appaloosa with large black spots led the herd around the field before rearing. I stopped my car to take a few shots of him. He was magnificent. As I continued up the drive, my car bumped through the last pothole before pulling up to the wraparound porch at our family's home. I grabbed my cameras, laptop, and duffle bag and climbed up the steps.

Mama was in the kitchen. Pots and pans clanked together in the sink. A pot of chili bubbled on the stove.

"That smells delicious." I grabbed a spoon from the dish rack by the sink and swiped some chili. The spicy chili and garlic flavor burst over my tongue. I groaned. I missed Texas chili.

"Katie!" Mama set down her knife and turned it to me. "I didn't even hear you pull in." She crossed the kitchen to wrap me in a large hug. "It's been too long since you've been home."

"I know, Mama." The guilt inside my chest bubbled just like the chili in the pot on the stove.

She held me back at arm's length inspected me from head to toe. "You've changed a lot since from that Gothic teenager I sent to college." She smiled and her eyes were shining with unshed tears. She pulled me back into her embrace. "Oh how, I've missed you."

We stayed like that for a few minutes. Tears prickled in the corners of my eyes. I missed my Mama, too. Being home was comfortable. The smell of chili and cornbread filled the kitchen and my heart. I loved my parents and I could never tell them that I needed to go away for myself. I needed to prove to myself I could be successful on my own. I had to free myself from the anxiety that crippled me most of my life. The only way to do that was to throw myself into a life that was different from the ranch and Sunnydale.

Mama went back to cutting up cornbread. "Tell me, how is Denver treating you?"

"It's good." I shrugged. "I've several pieces in galleries around Colorado, but you know that. Did you get the email with the pictures I sent you?"

"I did. Your daddy and I are very proud of you." She beamed at me from the counter. "And that is why I'm not surprised that Annie asked you to take pictures of her wedding."

The smile on my face drooped at the mention of what I had to do this evening. She noticed and patted my hand.

"You'll do well. I'm sure of it. We've been bragging to all of our friends about our famous daughter, the photographer."

A blush crept up my neck. Unshed tears escaped my eyes and rolled down my cheeks.

"Thank you, Mama," I hugged her again.

"You should probably go see your daddy before you go back to town. He's in the barn with Kaleb feeding the horses."

I set my things down in my room, kissed her on the cheek as I went back through the kitchen, and snagged a hunk of cornbread on my way to the barn.

The barn door swung open with a creak. Some things never changed. Daddy was sitting at his desk in the office, pounding away on his keyboard. I made my way down the barn aisle. A soft white nose nudged me as I walked past her stall.

"Buttercup!"

Her whiskers tickled the palm of my hand as I fed her the rest of the piece of cornbread. She lipped my hand looking for more and nickered a throaty sound. Her big brown eyes pierced my soul.

"Don't be greedy. I'll bring you some carrots tomorrow morning." I whispered into her ear.

I proceeded down to his office and knocked on the door frame. Daddy was a big man with a full head of grey hair that was bleached white by the sun. His skin showed the evidence that he'd worked outside every day of his life. Seeing my family for the first time in years, drug up emotions I hadn't felt in a long time. Again, tears swam in my eyes when he looked up. A giant smile broke across his face and he hurried around his desk.

"Baby! My world traveler is home." He wrapped me into a bear hug that lifted my feet off the hard-packed clay.

"Daddy, I've missed you so much." I buried my face in his red flannel shirt. He smelled of fresh-cut hay and horses. After a minute, he set me down.

"Let me see you." He stepped back and looked me up and down. "My little girl has all grown up." His voice got rougher as he patted the top of my head. His eyes were bright with tears.

"Daddy, don't do that I am going to cry." I wiped at a lone tear rolling down my cheek.

"What's with all the crying?" A deep male voice sounded behind me.

"Kaleb!" I launched myself at my oldest brother. He was as tall and broad as my daddy but his hair was blonde and curly like mine. It stuck out at odd angles underneath his cowboy hat. His dark blue eyes twinkled as he swung me around.

"The little brat has finally decided to come home." He set me down and ruffled the top of my head.

"I'm not a brat." I playfully punched him on the arm.

"Ouch." He rubbed the bicep I hit with a fake frown on his face. "I'm telling Mom." I rolled my eyes at him and he winked back at me.

"Your momma said that Annie talked you into being the wedding photographer." Daddy said.

"Yah," I looked at the toe of my sandal and scuffed it in the dirt. When I looked up, both men were looking at me. They had their arms crossed and were leaning against the wall, exact mirror images of each other. My cheeks flushed and my heart raced. "I don't do people." I threw my hands up in the air. "My photography is all landscapes and nature. What if I blow it?"

"Baby, you're going to do great. You plan everything out. It's just your anxiety kicking in." Daddy smiled at me softly.

"Levi said something like that earlier today." I pushed my hair out of my face.

"He's right." Daddy said. "I'd better go get ready for this shindig as I'm the one marrying those two love birds." He squeezed my shoulder as he walked past. "I'm happy you're home, Baby."

An awkward silence filled the barn until the door swung shut, leaving me and Kaleb sharing the same space. He regarded me with a weird expression on his face. I glanced around the small office and turned to leave

"Wait a minute." Kaleb broke in. "When did you see Levi?"

"Annie assigned him as my assistant."

Kaleb leveled a glare that caused me to blush under his scrutiny. He leaned toward me. "Stay away from him, Katie." He whispered in my ear.

"Why? He's your best friend." I whispered back. *How dare he tell me who I am going to hang out with!* Heat rose up my neck and ears. *What was he talking about?*

"And I know him better than most. He's not the type to have a steady girlfriend. I don't want to kill my best friend when he breaks your heart." He growled before storming away.

Chapter 4

Katie

By the time I'd changed into a pair of slacks and an unwrinkled blouse, I was running late. My car swung into the parking lot of the chapel. Several other cars were already there. Silhouettes of people flitted by the windows as I made my way inside. I slowly opened the door, silently praying not to be noticed.

"Finally, Katie is here." Annie marched toward me and dragged me into the room.

All the eyes turned on me as heat flushed my face. I gave a small wave to the crowd. Luckily, everyone was busy getting ready for the ceremony run through.

"We are going to do a brief run-through. I want you to take some candid shots, but nothing too overboard and then we are going to Cowboy's for dinner. You don't have to come to that." She said without taking a breath.

"Cowboy's, the bar?" *Really, a rehearsal dinner at the only bar in town?* My eyebrow raised at her.

"It's the only place in Sunnydale that serves food and my mom didn't want to host people at our house."

I nodded in understanding. "They do have some good food."

"Alright, folks." My daddy called from the front of the chapel, clapping his hands together. "Let's get this show on the road. I'm sure you're all hungry."

Everyone cheered. Annie herded and directed people where she wanted them to go. Someone hit play on a stereo and an organ chord floated on the air. Annie stood in front like an orchestra director, waving at people. She cupped her hands over her mouth and shouted.

"Levi, bring Mom and Granny down the aisle."

All eyes turned to the back of the church where he stood with a woman on each arm. My throat tightened when his eyes searched for mine. He looked dashing in dark washed Wranglers, polished cowboy boots, and his hair was combed down. He led them down the aisle in a slow march. Granny was pushing ninety and shuffled very slowly. Her thick gray hair was tied into a bun at the base of her head and an ivory shawl covered her shoulders. Their mother was on his other arm. She stood a head shorter than Levi. She was wearing a silver dress that highlighted the silver highlights in her black waist-length hair she was beaming at Annie and Levi in turn. Annie and Levi had been raised by a single mom. Even though things were hard at times, they loved each other and it showed. My heart filled with love watching the exchange of the small family.

Once everyone was seated, the bridal party marched to the front of the chapel. After that, the rehearsal of the service went by quickly with Daddy saying a few words and Annie and Bobby responding in turn. Everyone clapped at the end just like at the real wedding. Bobby and Annie stared into each other's eyes for a long moment but did not kiss. I snapped a few photos here and there but overall, I lost myself in the enjoyment of the occasion.

"Thank you so much." Annie wrapped me into a hug. "It means so much to me to have everything documented. I can't tell you enough how much I appreciate you." She stepped back from me and gave me a once over. "You look beat. Why don't you go home and spend some time with your family?"

I caught Levi watching me from over in the corner. His eyes burned with an intensity I hadn't seen before. Suddenly, I was tired and needed some space.

"You're right. I'm exhausted." I faked a yawn and slipped out of the room before he made his way over to me.

Levi

I helped Mom and Granny into my truck to go to Cowboy's Bar. The cab was cozy with three people in the front seat, but it was nice. The women chatted about everything that still needed to be done and all of the plans for tomorrow. I was able to zone out and think about the woman with curly blond hair and curves in all the right places. The one that didn't realize how special and talented she was.

"What are you smiling at?" Mom broke into my thoughts.

Granny tisked. "He's daydreaming of the little Kisment girl. Any fool can see that."

I rubbed my hand up the back of my neck as my ears burned. Leave it to Granny to see things as they were.

"She's a cutie. And Annie is always raving about how good her photography is." Mom checked her make-up in the mirror.

"We're here." I turned my truck into the gravel lot and pulled up to the door of the bar. A sigh left me as Mom and Granny climbed out.

MY COWBOY CRUSH

"She's a special one. Don't break her heart." Granny whispered before being led inside the bar.

Man, I couldn't catch a break. I swung my truck around and found an empty spot in the back.

The bar was expecting us. Lindsay, the waitress, ushered us to a large room at the back of the bar away from the patron. We sat down at a long table and water glasses were placed in front of us. Lindsay came back a few minutes later to take our orders. She started at the head of the table where Annie and Bobby sat and went around. Mom, Granny, and I were last to place our orders. Today, she wore a black leather mini skirt, red tank top, and high-heeled boots that went up to her knees. Her blond hair twisted into a French braid that went down her back.

"Hi handsome, what would you like to eat today?" She placed her hand onto my shoulder and gently rubbed circles on my back.

I knew Lindsay for a long time. She just wasn't my type. She liked to flirt and wanted attention from any man. Every time I frequented at Cowboy's Bar, she tried and tried and tried to get me to interact with her. But the only blonde girl that I was interested in, was the one that was off-limits. The one that starred in my dreams at night and during the day. It didn't matter what I was doing, I could be checking fence at the ranch and my thoughts would stray to Katie. I shrugged off her hand nonchalantly.

"A bacon burger and fries would be just fine, thank you."

"Will do." she winked at me before heading to the kitchen with her orders. I groaned inwardly, I wish she would take a hint.

Dinner went by fast with lots of laughing, lots of talking, and excitement about the wedding coming up. I hadn't spent a lot of time with Bobby's family. We both worked at the ranch together but his family flew in from California. They told stories about Bobby riding his horse in the mountains, crashing his first car, and skinny dipping at the school's pool. They were great people and would be a welcome addition to our little family. It was just Annie, Mom, and me. Our dad disappeared several years ago when we were both little, leaving Mom to raise twins by herself. So little that we don't remember him, and Mom never mentioned why he left. She spent all of her time being a single mom working full-time and trying to make us happy. She sat with a big smile plastered on her face as she listened to Bobby's parents joke and laugh. But I knew, she was hurting inside that she didn't have that. My heart broke for her.

As dinner came to a close, the sound of a steel guitar and drums floated through the open door. Annie and Bobby moved around the table thanking people and saying their goodnights. My boots tapped along with the tune the band played.

"Granny and I are heading out. Why don't you stay and have some fun with your sister and your new brother-in-law to be? Bobby's parents are going to take us home." Mom patted my hand and then got up to help Granny out of her chair. I placed a kiss on both of their cheeks.

"I'll see you tomorrow. I love you."

Mom squeezed my hand, a small smile spread across her lips. "I love you too."

The band played country songs with a couple of guitars, a drum, and a fiddle. The crowd was on their feet stomping, swaying, and turning to the old country tunes. A line dance formed with hoots and hollers on the small sawdust-covered floor. I slid onto an empty barstool at the bar. Lindsay came up and set a full glass of beer in front of me.

"I get off in five. Will you still be here?" She batted her eyelashes at me.

"Planning on it." I took a swig from my beer. The coldness shocked my mouth but felt good sliding down my throat, taking the distaste out of my mouth.

Lindsay moved on to the next customer to take their order. On the dance floor, Annie and Bobby were two-stepping around. He held her close and she beamed as they made their way around the line dance. They looked good together. *Will I ever find someone that I'd feel that way about? Could Katie be the one for me?* I took another pull of my beer. Bar stools on either side of me screeched as they were pulled out. My friends, Pete and Damien, sat on each side of me. Pete was an engineer at the factory in town. He'd just moved back to work his grandfather's ranch. Damien worked security for a big firm in San Antonio. He'd spent years in the military and he looked like it.

"Are you tired of working for the Kisments, yet?" Pete nodded to the bartender for a beer.

A laugh started deep in my belly and spilled out of my mouth. It was an ongoing joke between us.

"I could offer you a real good deal." Pete sipped his beer.

"Really? What kind of deal can you offer me today?"

Pete scratched his head, looking like he was thinking hard. "I could pay you about a penny an hour. That's probably twice what you're making over at the ranch."

A snort erupted from my throat. "Oh yeah, that's like three times what I'm making at the ranch."

We both laughed. Every time I met Pete, he offered me a job but he had no money to pay me. It would still be several years before he got his ranch off of the ground. And, maybe just maybe, then he could afford to pay me to be his ranch manager. Damien shook his head at our exchange before drinking his beer.

A few minutes later, Lindsay approached. She nodded to Pete and Damien before turning to me. Pete and Lindsay have an on-again/off-again relationship. Obviously, they must be on the off tonight. She leaned in toward me.

"Cowboy, I'm done with my shift. About time you swung me around on that dance floor."

I didn't feel like dancing, but when a pretty girl asks you to dance my mama taught me to tell them yes. I nodded to Damien and Pete before leading Lindsay out into the boot stopping crowd. The band switched to a fast country song. I swung her around and grasped her waist with one hand and led her into a quick two-step as we circled the dance floor. Lindsay was a pretty girl with her long hair and tight clothes but I found my mind wandering. *What it would feel like to have Katie in my arms instead of her?* We spun around and around for a couple more songs. As the crowd clapped when the band finished for their break, I stepped back from Lindsay's embrace.

"I'd better be going." I faked a yawn and looked at my watch. "The sun comes up early on the ranch." I tipped my hat to her. "Thank you for the dance." I turned on my heel and headed toward the door. She grabbed my hand as I reached for the doorknob.

"I'll be more than happy to go with you," she purred, "to keep your bed warm for you tonight." She fluttered her big green eyes at me. "Come on, cowboy. I want to know if the rumors are true."

"What rumors?" I narrowed my gaze at her.

"Oh, you know," she winked.

Bile rose in my throat as my stomach clenched. A coldness crept into my voice as I flung her hand off of mine. "Those aren't true."

I stalked to my truck, leaving her in the doorway of the bar. The cool night air slapped my cheeks and drove all thought of tonight from my mind. I climbed into my truck, heading back to the ranch, all the while thinking about the one blond girl that I didn't dance with tonight.

Katie

A rooster crowing woke me from my sleep. For a moment, I was confused as to where I was. I haven't heard roosters in the five years since I've left home. There weren't too many in Denver. I rolled over in my twin size bed and shoved the pink comforter to the floor. Stretching my arms above my head, I rolled my head from side to side. It was going to be a beautiful day for Annie's wedding.

The noise of banging pots and pans came from the kitchen as the scent of coffee permeated the air. Sudden inspiration struck. I grabbed an old pair of boots and jeans and threw on a cotton t-shirt. With my old camera, that was a gift from my grandparents, slung over my neck and a cowboy hat pulled down to my eyes, I made my way to the front door.

"Morning, sunshine." Mama's happy voice halted my escape from the house.

"Hi, Mama."

"Where you out to?"

"Just taking Buttercup for a ride. The sunrise should be beautiful this morning."

"Breakfast is in an hour." She turned back to whatever was in the pot on the stove.

"I'll be back I promise."

I ran down the creaky steps, across the dew-covered grass, and into the barn. The horses slept quietly in their stalls as I swung Buttercup's stall door open. I brushed and saddled her quickly, anxious to be on my way. I was about to throw a leg over her back when a voice clearing stopped me in my tracks.

"You going out without me?" Levi's deep voice sent shivers down my spine.

I turned slowly to him. Looking at him made my mouth water. His black shaggy hair stood up in all directions and his gray eyes looked deep into mine. He slapped a dusty hat against his faded blue jeans before shoving it on his head. The butterflies in my stomach rolled over at the sight of his T-shirt stretching across his chest muscles. They flexed as he crossed his arms. Yummy. I shook my head to clear my thoughts.

"I was going out without anyone."

"Then, you won't mind if I join you."

He quickly saddled a black horse on the end of the barn and swung into the saddle with the ease of a gymnast. I clambered onto Buttercup's back, feeling self-conscious of my awkwardness. A small smile played upon his lips as I struggled into the saddle.

"I could've given you a boost."

"Nah, I'm good." I straightened my spine and pulled my hat down even closer to my ears.

"Lead the way," he said.

I clucked to Buttercup and squeezed her with my legs. She started at a swinging walk. The air was brisk before the sun began its rise. The chill caused goosebumps to run up and down my arms, and I shivered involuntarily against the cold. I caught him looking at me with concern in his eyes.

"I'm fine," I muttered and turned Buttercup on the trail that led out to the range.

"Still, I might be cold. Let's stop at the bunkhouse." He rubbed his arms and shook, slightly.

He turned off onto a beaten trail that led to the bunkhouse. It was a small brown building that held eight apartments. He dashed inside and he banged around for a while. He came out with a beat-up leather jacket slung over his shoulder.

"Put this on. I'm not watching you shiver." He handed me the jacket.

I slid my arms into the worn-out sleeves. It smelled like him, horse sweat, leather, and something spicy that can only be man. I snuggled into it, pulling the collar up. He was right it was warmer than my t-shirt. He mounted his horse and motioned for me to lead the way.

We rode for a while in silence, enjoying that part of the day that wasn't quite morning and wasn't quite night, when everything was still quiet and gray. Owls hooting in the distance. Jackrabbits scurried through the underbrush. A hawk took off from a mesquite tree and flew overhead. The sun started to peek over the horizon. The sky streaked with reds, purples, and blues. It was a beauty I hadn't seen in a while. We stopped at the top of a hill. I dismounted and handed my reins to Levi.

"If you needed to come along. Make yourself useful."

I set up my camera to capture the sunrise. Levi stood behind me, keeping quiet as I worked. His gaze felt heavy on my back and wondered what he was thinking. After twenty minutes of laying on the sandy ground, I tried to stand up. Levi's boots crunched over small stones as he moved to help me up. His fingers threaded with mine as he jerked me to my feet. I ended up nose to nose with him. My breath caught in my throat as his grey eyes captured mine. His eyes grew darker the longer I stared into his. His warm spicy breath came in short puffs across my face. His arms slid around my shoulders and back, bringing me closer to him. My pulse hammered in my ears. It was hard to breathe, think, and even stand. I leaned into him. His head tilted toward mine. His lips came within a hair's breadth from mine. I closed my eyes and leaned forward. At that moment, Buttercup walked up behind me and nudged me in the back with her nose. I jerked forward, hitting Levi in the chin. My lip caught between my teeth as a little blood trickled down from the split in my lip. Levi's strong hands set me back onto my feet.

"Buttercup's right." He dabbed at my lip with the edge of his T-shirt. My skin tingled where he touched it. "I'm sure breakfast is almost ready."

A moment passed between us. I wanted to kiss him, but he turned to get the horses ready to ride back home. He led Buttercup over to me and offered his hands down by the stirrup. I placed my worn-out cowboy boot in his hand and he lifted me into the saddle. I settled into my seat as he mounted his horse. We turned to make the trek back to the house. The silence stretched between us as nature awoke. Birds sang in the bushes, crickets chirped, and armadillos waddled back to their homes. My camera clicked away at the wildlife.

"What's with the camera?" Levi broke the silence as he watched me try to focus in on a roadrunner.

"Whatcha mean?" I mumbled as I leaned more out of the saddle for a different angle.

"That camera is older and smaller than the one you had yesterday. In fact, it doesn't look digital at all."

I straightened in the saddle and held the camera out from my body. "It is different. This was my first camera, ever. My grandparents gave it to me." I choked up at the thought of both of them. They've been gone for several years and I missed them a bunch. I wiped the single tear from my eye and straightened my spine in the saddle. I steered Buttercup down the trail to the house.

"So, why do you use it?" Levi rode his horse up next to me.

"Well, because I like it." I snapped a few more pictures. "I think the film takes better pictures than digital. There's just something about being in a dark room, developing the film, watching the picture come to life." I shrugged before continuing down the trail.

"You have your own darkroom?" Levi trotted his horse next to me.

"Yep. Sure do."

"Really?"

I nodded my head. "I set one up in the closet at my apartment. That way I can develop my film whenever I want and I don't have to send it out. It really isn't a big deal."

Silence fell between us as we traveled the rest of the way to the ranch house. When we pulled up into the yard, the rest of my family and all the ranch hands were gathered.

"Breakfast time, y'all," Mama called from the porch. Everyone cheered.

Levi grabbed the reins of Buttercup's bridle as I dismounted. "You might as well go in and get some breakfast. I'll take care of the horses for you. I'd better get going to town anyway, as I'm sure Annie's got a bunch of stuff for me to do."

I couldn't help but watch him walk away. His jeans hugged his hips and butt. I closed my mouth with a snap. His boots clicked on the gravel as he made his way into the barn. I turned around to see the glare coming off of Kaleb's eyes. He shook his head at me before heading into the house. The next few hours might be interesting.

Levi

The horses plodded after me as I headed to the barn. The barn door groaned as I slid it open and let the morning light fall across the dirt-covered floor. Horses' heads popped over their stall doors and nickered as I led Buttercup and my black horse to their stalls.

"Give me a second, everyone. I've gotta untack these two, and then it's breakfast." I said out loud to the barn.

The horses answered with neighs, banging on stall doors, and general restlessness. I tied the two horses up and took off their saddles. They weren't sweaty from our morning ride, so a nice brushing would be sufficient. I hummed a tune under my breath as I ran the brush over Buttercup's copper coat. This morning was perfect. The sunset was gorgeous, and the girl with me was just as beautiful. The kiss would've been perfect if we hadn't been interrupted. Her soft lips gently touching mine, maybe she would cling to my body as I wrapped her even closer to me. The scent of her perfume lingered over the smell of horses. The brush flicked dust off of Buttercup's rump when a throat clearing brought me back to the present. I knew that sound, my hand stilled, and my body slowly turned to the man standing behind me.

Kaleb's arms crossed over his chest and his feet braced shoulder-width apart. His cowboy hat was squashed tight over his ears and the blond curls stuck out underneath of it. His eyes turned an angry midnight blue and a muscle ticked in his jaw.

"Morning, didn't see you there." I tried to seem nonchalant, but my heart was racing. I had just broken rule number three at the Kisment Ranch, but nothing happened...unfortunately.

"What do you think you're doing?" The anger in his tone didn't surprise me. Kaleb had always been protective of his baby sister.

"Brushing down the horses before feeding the barn." I waved the brush around and grinned at him.

His eyes got darker as he swore under his breath. "No," he ground his teeth together, "what were you doing with Katie?"

His hands dropped to his sides and balled into fists. I stepped a small step back and leaned against the wall. *What had I been doing with Katie? Definitely not what I wanted to do with Katie.* I picked up a piece of straw and twirled it between my fingers.

"Katie was going for a morning ride, and I joined her." He growled the moment the words left my mouth. I held up my hands. "Honestly, man, it was just a ride to get some sunrise photos and nothing else."

He relaxed a little and leaned toward me. "Stay away from her. She doesn't need a broken heart."

It was my turn to cross my arms and study him. "What makes you think I am going to break her heart?"

He threw his head back and laughed but it didn't reach his eyes. "You're my best friend."

"Aw, how sweet."

"But the ladies call you 'Love 'em n' Leave 'em Levi'. Just don't hurt my sister." He turned and stomped out of the barn, just as the words died on my tongue.

But that's not the real me.

Chapter 5

Katie

"Hey, honey, what are you doing?" Mama braced her hand on the doorway. "Are you ready for the big day?"

I nodded. And double-checked my list. "Can you help me go over this?"

"Sure," she said, "Camera."

"Check." I packed the large professional camera in my bag.

"Memory card."

"Check."

"Extra memory card."

"Check."

"Notebook."

"Check."

"Laptop, extra batteries, extra lenses."

"Got it."

"Well, honey, I think you've got everything."

I packed it all into my backpack and slung it over my shoulder. Nervous butterflies danced in my stomach. I pushed a stray curl behind my ear and looked around my pink room.

"Well Mama, this room has not changed in the five years I've been gone."

She chuckled. "No, I couldn't bear to make it into a room of my own. I left all of your stuff here in case you ever decided to come back and stay at the ranch."

I glanced over at her as she choked up on the last words of the sentence. Tears ran down the edge of her cheek.

"Oh Mama, don't cry." I stepped across the pink plush rug and wrapped her into a hug.

I never realized how much Mama and Daddy missed me. And at that moment, I missed them too. I missed Texas and I missed being on the ranch. I loved Colorado, my friends out there, my job, and my apartment. The mountains were beautiful; they took my breath away every time I saw them. It hit me that I missed my family. My eyes filled up with tears. Mama held me out at arm's length and wiped the tear that escaped from my eye.

"Now, don't you be crying on me? You're going to ruin your mascara." She dabbed at it and fixed my makeup. "Well, you better be going, girl. You're going to be late for the wedding."

I chuckled as I glanced at my watch. The wedding didn't start until two o'clock, and it was only nine in the morning.

"Well, I probably should get going so I can catch all the preparations." I held up my notebook. "She wants a lot of pictures."

Mama laughed with me, "that Annie sure knows how to put on a party."

The park pavilion parking lot was full of cars and trucks by the time I arrived. Annie stuck her head out through the door when she heard my truck pull up.

"Katie, you're finally here! Hurry up, we've got a lot going on."

Anxiety grew in my stomach. It rolled around causing the butterflies to twist and turn. Nausea rose in my throat. I gave a small wave to Annie. She waved back before heading back inside. The door clicked shut behind her. *Breathe in, Katie, breathe out.* My head rested on the steering wheel, trying to calm the butterflies in my stomach.

A knock sounded at my window. Levi grinned down at me through the window.

"Are you ok?" He opened my door and gently set his hand on my back, sending tingles down my spine.

"Just having a panic attack." My voice wheezed.

"Breathe in and out. You'll do great." He rubbed my back in slow circles. His voice calming my frayed nerves. I smiled weakly at him.

"Thank you." I reached for my bag and my hand shook when I clutched my backpack and camera.

"You've got this, Katie," his voice washed over me, "breathe in, breathe out."

I breathed in through my mouth and out through my nose, holding for 3 seconds, trying to reach that elusive calm. I repeated the cycle five times until the butterflies in my stomach calmed to a gentle fluttering instead of a crazy rock and roll party. I exited my truck and he grabbed the rest of my equipment before heading towards the park pavilion. Loud voices, exuberant cries, and laughter burst through the door as we reached it. He stepped in front of me and opened the door. He smiled down at me as he placed his hand on my lower back. His grey eyes widened and glinted silver. The butterflies swooned. *Get yourself together, Katie.* I could get lost in those eyes.

Tables and chairs were set up for dinner after the wedding. A banquet table was set up along the outside wall and the head table was up on risers in front of the gathering of other tables. One of the bridesmaids stuck her head out of a side room and waved at me.

"We're in here!"

I strolled across the concrete floor. Breathing in, breathing out, my hands shaking, palms sweating. I was pretty sure my perfume was wearing off. My eye makeup felt like it was sliding down my face. I grasped Levi's hand. A nervous sweat broke out when I walked into the room. The fumes of hairspray, makeup, and other beauty products assaulted my nose. A sneeze erupted and I blushed as all of their gazes fell on me.

"Bless you," Levi whispered in my ear. A shiver passed through me.

Someone pushed a mimosa into my hand. Annie and her bridesmaids were in various stages of getting ready. At that moment, one was having her hair primped and curled to be done up into a fancy up-do. Annie's mom sat on a couch on the side, getting her make-up done. Granny squealed with delight as the manicurist painted her nails a brilliant red.

"Katie," Annie startled me. My mimosa splashed over the size of the champagne flute. "I want you to take pictures of everyone. I want to be able to see the whole day when I page through the photo album."

"Hold still," the stylist scolded. Annie flashed me a smile and made the motion of taking pictures with her fingers.

The butterflies quieted. I guess candid shots it was. I glanced around, but Levi disappeared. I shrugged, time to get to work. I went around the room, taking pictures of the girls getting ready, trying to keep it modest and appropriate to be seen by Granny. Eventually, the time came for Annie to slip into her dress. I took pictures of her mother helping her button the tiny white buttons that ran up the back. Silhouette shots of her standing in the window looking out across the park and the girls helping her put on her garter. As they were helping her slip on her shoes, a knock sounded on the door frame.

"Levi," Annie's mom called, "you brought the flowers. That's wonderful." She rushed forward, hustling Levi into the room, and distributed the flowers to the girls.

"Here, honey, take some pictures of the flowers." She pushed me to the front of the room.

Levi smiled at me from underneath his hat. A flush spread through me as I lined the girls up to take pictures of the bouquets with the dresses.

"All right, ladies," I said, "let's go outside and take some pictures in the garden. We have about an hour before I have to spend time with the groom and the groomsmen."

We all trooped out to the garden where I took pictures of the bride's wedding party underneath the trees, around by the flowers, in the tall grass by the cacti. They held funny poses and serious poses all the while Levi stood behind me holding the light shade. My body tingled with awareness when his eyes fell on me. I shivered as if I was showered in ice. He tried to catch my eye, but I ignored him. Once in a while, my eyes slipped to the side and found him staring at me with a small grin creasing his face or he'd wink back. It was hard to focus on the bride and bridesmaids. The handsome cowboy was affecting my concentration.

"Alright, ladies. Let's take some photos by the rose arch. Annie, I want you to be seated on the bench. And, girls, I want you to be standing behind her." I directed everyone where to stand.

The arch of red roses looked lovely with Annie's white wedding dress and her girls' pale pink bridesmaids' dresses. At the angle, it was just not right.

"Levi, can you stand over there to left?"

He stepped away from behind me and took three strides over to the left. He raised the light over his head. My nose wrinkled and I shook my head. It still was not the right angle. I looked over at the fountain behind me. The rock wall sat up about a foot from the ground. It was rough on the surface, but I think if I stood upon it, I would get a better angle. I swept the camera strap around my neck and set the camera against my chest. I climbed up onto the rock wall. I focused on the screen as I took a step to the right. My foot slipped on the rock; my arms flailed as I fell backward into the fountain.

Levi

I watched Katie all morning. She sure was cute with her Gypsy skirt and white blouse. She wore these ridiculous flats with little bows on the toes. The minute she stepped onto the rock; my heart dropped in my chest. My feet stepped toward her as she took a step to her right. Her foot hit the rock, and she fell backward with a large splash into the water. I raced towards her.

"Katie, are you okay?" I peered into the water.

Her blonde hair hung limp around her face. Her mascara smeared on her eyelids and ran down her cheeks. Her white blouse became see-through. I drug my eyes up from the blouse to stare at her eyes. Her skin turned a gray pale color, and she was opening and closing her mouth like a fish out of water.

"Here, let me help you up?" I grasped her hand to pulled her out of the water. Her long skirt clung to her body and she stepped up over the edge of the rock wall.

"Oh no," she cried, "my camera it's ruined!"

Tears slid down her face as she looked at her camera dangling by its neck cord. It broke my heart to see her crying. I wrapped my arms around her and pulled her to me, rubbing circles on her back.

"Everything will be alright," I soothed.

"What am I going to do? I won't be able to take pictures for Annie!" She sobbed into my shoulder.

Annie approached. "Well, the first thing you need to do is go get changed. I'll have my girls fix your hair and makeup in no time. We'll postpone the wedding for about half an hour, so you'll have time to go home shower and come back."

"Really? You would do that all for me?" She hiccupped and wiped at the mascara.

Annie chuckled. "Of course, you're the little sister I never wanted." She patted Katie's arms and went back to her girls. Someone poured another round of mimosas.

I turned to Katie. "Let me take you home."

Her teeth clacked together even though it was July in Texas. I took my suit jacket off and wrapped it around her shoulders. I ushered her to my truck. Part of me felt bad for what happened to Katie; the other part was grateful for some time alone with her. I opened the door and helped her in. She seemed to zone out, so I buckled her seat belt for her and closed the door. I climbed in and started the truck. The engine rumbled to life.

"It'll be all right," I assured her, "you'll see." Silence filled the cab of the truck as we drove a while. A lightbulb went off in my head.

"Why don't you use the camera you had this morning?"

She turned her eyes to me. They were red-rimmed and black mascara streaked down her cheeks.

"But that's a film camera. I won't have enough film to take all the pictures Annie wants."

I drummed my fingers on the steering wheel as we pulled into the Kisment Ranch. "What if we stopped at the store and bought a bunch of disposable cameras? That way the people at the wedding reception can take pictures of their tables for Annie. You can focus on just the ceremony and the before and after shots."

She turned her tear-soaked face to me and smiled. "I guess, we can do that."

She tucked a strand of blonde hair behind her ear as she reached for the door handle. "Give me a few seconds to shower and change. I'll be right back."

She jumped up out of the truck and ran to the house, dripping water all the way there. The screen door slammed behind her. I smiled to myself as I reached in the backseat and grabbed the towel. I wiped up the seat where she was sitting. I gave Katie my suit jacket. My white shirt and tie looked silly with my black pants. I sighed. *I guess I'll have to go change.* I got out of the truck and walked down to the bunkhouse. I pulled on a pair of black Wrangler jeans and a button-up western shirt, tied a bolo around my neck, and set my new black hat on my head. It was after Memorial Day so I should've worn a white hat. Mom taught me better, but I hated my white straw hat. Annie would just have to get over it. I headed back out to the truck.

Katie leaned against the railing of the porch, ringing out her wet hair. She changed into skinny jeans that hugged all of her curves and a bright blue top that made her blue eyes pop. When she glanced at me, her mouth opened and closed a couple of times.

"Wow, that's different." A rosy tint colored her cheeks.

"Like different how?" I leaned up against the porch railing on the other side of her and a slow smile twitched at my lips.

"Like you look really good." Even her ears turned pink.

"I know I looked good in my suit," I tipped my hat back and rubbed at my forehead.

"Well, you did look good in your suit but you look really good right now." She stared down at her boots. She twisted her hair up into some sort of a knot on the top of her head and held it in place with a large metal hairpin. She had a camera bag slung over her shoulder and her hand gripped her purse.

"I'm ready if you are? Everybody seems to already be at the park." She made her way down the steps and I grasped her hand to help her. My skin tingled the minute her fingers touched mine and my heart raced. She looked beautiful.

"Katie."

"Yeah?" She turned her eyes to me. The blue in her eyes was just as blue as a cloudless sky.

"You look very pretty."

She snorted and looked the other way. "Yeah, like pretty as a drowned rat." She hurried over to the truck. I shook my head. What I wouldn't give for her to realize that I meant that she looks beautiful to me.

We stopped at the pharmacy and the Dollar Store just outside of town. I found a couple of disposable cameras but no extra film.

"How much do you have?" I glanced over to her.

She went through her camera bag. "I have about 20 rolls."

"That's a lot." This was me trying to make conversation.

She shrugged. Her horrible anxiety must be back, and that must be what she's dealing with right now. Her knees shook, her hand tapped on the edge of the window, and she was barely breathing. The pink drained from her cheeks, and she kept twirling her hair with her other hand.

"It will be fine, I promise you. Annie will be more than happy for everything that you've done." I laid my hand on her bouncing knee.

"What if the pictures are no good? What if I don't get the exposure right? What if their eyes are closed? What if no one's smiling or what if someone is in the wrong spot? I can't just hit delete and do it over again!"

I parked my truck before I took her hands in mine and rubbed my thumb over her knuckles. "It'll be alright. Photographers have been taking pictures of weddings for a lot longer than digital cameras have been around. You can do this and Annie thinks you can do this. Plus, you got the memory card from the digital camera. That should still work."

She nodded, "I've got to run and take the groomsmen pictures."

"I'll see you at the beginning of the wedding."

She leaned toward me as I leaned into her. Her pink lips pressed a light kiss on my cheek before she jumped out of the truck and ran to where Bobby and his men were hanging out underneath an oak tree.

The wedding was supposed to go off at two o'clock. Annie had pushed it back a little bit so that Katie could get some more pictures. People arrived to be seated and Annie made me an usher. I seated Mom and Granny at the front of the church. Bobby's parents sat on the other side. Bobby appeared in his tuxedo, walking among the guests, shaking hands, and talking to them. My body focused on Katie in the corner, taking pictures of the altar, her dad reading the Bible. Our eyes met across the room. I tipped my hat to her. She smiled and dropped her eyes back down to her camera.

A hand slid into the crook of my elbow, drawing my attention away from Katie as she concentrated into her camera.

"Would you like to find me a seat, cowboy?" Lindsay purred into my ear. I stifled a cringe and closed my eyes for a moment.

"Sure, Lindsay, why don't you come this way?"

I led her down the aisle to the fifth row from the front where one of my cousins sat. She wouldn't let go of my arm; instead, she ran her fingers from the tip of my elbow down into my hand and intertwined them with my fingers. My anger rose in my chest as I tried to keep it in check. I swallowed and let go of her fingers, but not before she pressed a kiss to the corner of my mouth.

"I can't wait for the dance later tonight," she whispered.

I just looked at her. My words were not forthcoming on what to respond. I turned to walk away. Her hand reached out to my bottom, giving it a firm squeeze. I narrowed my eyes at her, and my mouth opened, about to say something until Katie caught the corner of my eye. Her mouth fell open, and she was pale as a sheet. She finished snapping a couple of pictures before quickly hurrying away. When I made to go after her, I was interrupted by Kaleb. I groaned inwardly as he placed a hand on my shoulder.

"Good to see you, Levi. I missed you at breakfast." His dark blue eyes were unreadable.

I met his gaze and nodded. "Missed me at breakfast? I never went."

"Remember what I said." He strode away and found a seat next to his mom.

Crossing his arms, he stared ahead, his back straight as a ramrod. I ran my fingers through my hair and jammed my hat back on my head before heading to the back of the church.

The bells tolled, signaling the start of the wedding. The bridesmaids and Annie gathered behind the closed doors. Katie ran around them, snapping pictures. The world seemed to stop when I looked at Annie and her wedding dress. She was beautiful. Her black hair was swept up into ringlets to the white wedding dress showing off her tan. The veil laid over her eyes, but couldn't hide a little tear running down the side of her face. I caught it with my thumb and wiped it off.

"No crying today," I softly said to her, "it's supposed to be a happy day. You look amazing. Bobby's not going to know what hit him."

Annie beamed at me and threw her arms around me. At that moment it was just me and my sister. A sort of peace transcended us.

"Are you ready?"

Annie nodded. With that, I cued the pianist to play the processional. Her bridesmaids walked down the aisle, slowly smiling and nodding to friends and family that they knew. Katie was at the front. Her camera catching it all for Annie's memories. I offered Annie my elbow. She slipped her hand around my elbow. I wish our dad was here to see her. But he wasn't and I was proud to walk my sister down the aisle on the happiest day of her life to her new husband. The chapel doors swung open and everyone turned to look at us. We slowly stepped down the aisle together. My gaze swung to Katie and I gave her a small smile. She looked at me for a hard moment and went back to her camera. Her face was a blank mask like Kaleb's had been earlier.

Chapter 6

Katie

The wedding went as planned. Annie looked gorgeous in her wedding dress. Bobby's eyes bulged out of his head when he saw her. It was the perfect moment and I'm pretty sure I got it all on film. I had enough film to capture the whole wedding and pictures of the bride and groom together.

"Katie," Annie called to me from by the tree, "give that camera to Bobby. I want a picture with you and Levi."

Dread settled in my stomach as I handed the camera to Bobby. I slowly made my way over to Annie. But I couldn't say no to the bride as it was her special day. I looked horrible. My blonde hair had fallen from the bun I had twisted it into. My makeup was smeared, and I'm pretty sure I had grass stains on my skinny jeans. Not only that but the look that Lindsay had been giving Levi during the wedding played in flashes before my eyes. Kaleb warned me he was a playboy. It was my fault, letting my feelings getting the better of me. What was I thinking? I was just here for the weekend. How could I expect to try to change his ways? Why did I even care? My feet felt like bricks as I made my way over to Annie.

Levi had been trying to catch my eye since the wedding. He stood next to Annie, looking good in his button-up western shirt and black jeans. He held his cowboy hat in his hand. The other hand ran through his short black hair causing it to stand up on end. He gave me a small smile and worry colored his eyes. I took my place on the other side of Annie, wrapping my arm around her waist. We smiled at the camera. Bobby clicked a couple of pictures.

"I want one of my two favorite people." Annie stepped out from between us shoved us together.

My shoulder bumped into his side causing me to lose my balance. His arms wrapped around me to stop my fall. He pulled me upright and looked into my eyes. His gray eyes were stormy as they searched my soul. Time seemed to stretch between us. He slid his hand further around my waist, pulling me toward him. *Holy cow, he was going to kiss me.* In that second, his lips descended on mine. They were soft and sent sparks throughout my body. He slanted his head, driving the kiss deeper. Kissing Levi was everything I had ever thought it would be. My hands ran up his shoulders to grip his hair, and my left foot kicked out. A click sounded in the distance.

"Bummer, that was the last picture." Bobby sounded disappointed as we pulled apart.

Heat rushed to my face as the crowd erupted into cheers. I glanced over at Levi. The corners of his lips pulled up and he had not let me go. Anger welled up within me. How dare he kiss me when he was just flirting with Lindsay! Without thinking, my hand flew and connected with his cheek. His hands dropped from my waist, and he stepped back.

"What was that for?" His forehead wrinkled. He rubbed his cheek.

I rolled my eyes at him and put my hands on my hips. "Because you kissed me." I turned on my heel and stormed away.

My camera ran out of film, and I was done being the photographer for the wedding. I went back to being a guest. The wedding moved from the chapel to the park pavilion. My family sat at one of the tables close to the bride and groom. Levi's mom and his grandma sat at the table next to us. I found an open spot between Mamma and Kaleb and sat down.

"Are you okay?" Kaleb leaned over to me and put his arm around the back of my seat.

"Yep just fine."

"A woman is never fine when she says she's just fine." He smirked. "Do I need to beat him up for you?"

I shook my head. "No, he's just being Levi. We aren't together. He can flirt with whoever he wants." Bitterness colored my voice even though I tried to keep it out of it.

"I'm here for you, baby sister" He turned his attention back to the front as Annie and Bobby made their appearance. They both looked super happy as they gazed into each other's eyes as they made their way to the front table. Levi arrived not long after they did. His eyes bored into my back as he made his way to the table where his mom sat. He pulled out the chair behind me and lean towards me before he sat down.

"We need to talk."

I crossed my arms and ignored him. He sighed and sat down in his chair behind me.

"Lindsay!" His mom called. "You're sitting with us. There is an empty chair right next to Levi."

I ground my teeth together and try to plaster a fake smile on my face. Lindsay giggled and came over by Levi. He stood up like a gentleman and pulled out her chair for her. The chair scraped against the concrete floor as he pushed it in.

"Oh, that's so nice of you," her voice purred behind me. "Wasn't that a beautiful wedding?"

Levi grunted in response.

"I sure hope you save a dance for me tonight."

"Of course, I would love to dance with you tonight." I could feel his eyes burning holes in the back of my head.

I straightened my spine and swallowed a large gulp of water. Daddy stood up to say the prayer and everyone bowed their heads to murmur along with him. Levi's deep voice behind me drug my attention away from the prayer. Everyone chorused amen.

"Thank you, everyone, for coming to our wedding! We're so happy that you could share our special day with us. We'll start the buffet with the tables on the left. Get some food! Cheers!" Bobby raised his wine glass and toasted his wife before taking a drink. They gazed into each other's eyes as their lips slowly came together and they kissed. It made my heart ache, wishing this was something I could have. I wished it would be with the man behind me.

Levi

It was obvious. Katie was ignoring me. It probably had something to do with Lindsay's flirting but couldn't she see I did not initiate it. I wasn't even flirting back. My reputation ruined my chances with Katie. Frustration bubbled up within me. It was our table's turn to go through the buffet line. I hung back until our table had made it through and Katie's table was up. I handed her a plate as she stood in the line across the buffet table from me.

"Need anything from this side of the table?"

"No, thank you." The response was hard and fast.

I smiled at her but she glared at me before averting her gaze. She moved down the table. I grabbed some of the chicken fried steak, mashed potatoes and gravy, and a roll before heading back to my table. I didn't know how to make her pay attention to me. Maybe I read her wrong the whole weekend. I hoped not because my heart fell for her. Hard. I walked back to my table and sat down next to Lindsay and my mom.

"Levi, honey, Lindsay was just telling me about the ranch she inherited. She was saying that someday she might need a ranch manager."

Lindsay's eyes lit up as Mom and she discussed her new ranch. "I'll have to keep both of my jobs for a while. It's going to take a bit for it to turn a profit." She shrugged, laid her hand over mine. "I could use help whenever you're available."

I cut my gaze to her. She turned on a megawatt smile. Her eyes sparkled as she tried to get me to engage in their conversation.

"I don't know Lindsay, I'm pretty busy at the ranch."

"I'm sure the Kisments wouldn't mind if you came over on your days off."

I shrugged, hoping to get out of this conversation.

The dinner couldn't go by fast enough between Mom, Lindsay, and the girl behind me, ignoring me. I felt like I was drowning among women. Lindsay kept rubbing her foot against my leg and touching my hand with her hand. I gritted my teeth and tried not to lead her on. She was a nice girl and pretty to boot but my heart was still stuck on Katie.

The clinking of glasses brought my attention back to the front. Bobby and Annie stood together hand-in-hand.

"We'd like the speeches to begin, but first we want to thank someone very special." They raised their glasses towards Katie. "Without the lovely Katie here, we wouldn't have memories to show our children down the road." Annie leveled a gaze directly at Katie, an expression of softness covered her face. "Katie, I know how much you hate being the center of attention and how hard it was for you to do but we appreciate it from the bottom of our hearts. You've saved the day for us and gave us a perfect wedding."

They raised their glasses and toasted her. I swiveled in my seat and caught her profile as a blush crept up her neck. She averted her eyes to her plate and played with the ring on her fingers.

The rest of the evening went by fast after they did their toast. Eventually, we moved the tables and chairs to the side, arranging for the older folks to have somewhere to sit and talk while the younger people could dance. The country band set up in the corner. They started with some tunes. The lights dimmed, giving the room a fairytale feeling. Annie and Bobby danced the first dance. Then, it was the parent/child dance; since our father was gone, I stepped in and danced with Annie.

"Are you okay?" She whispered as we spun around the dance floor.

"Yeah," I didn't want to ruin her perfect day.

"That was quite a slap that Katie gave you earlier."

I dipped her and then swung her around.

"Whatever you did, at least you know she likes you."

"What do you mean by that?"

"How many girls have you kissed that slapped you?"

"None that I can think of."

Annie pulled away from me, a knowing look in her eye. "I think Katie likes you."

The song ended and we stepped apart. I rubbed my hand along the back of my neck and up through my hair. Annie thought that Katie liked me. That would be too good to be true. Bobby came and claimed Annie for the next dance, leaving me standing by myself in the middle of the dance floor. Teenagers and kids crowded on the floor when the band switched to an upbeat tune. I stepped through the crowd looking for Katie. Lindsay caught my eye and waved at me, pushing her way through the crowds toward me. *Well, Levi, you have to make a decision. Hurt Lindsay's feelings by turning her down or dance with Lindsay and hurt Katie even more.* I had a feeling with the looks that she and Kaleb gave me, that the reason they were upset was because of Lindsay's flirtations.

Lindsay caught my arm, "Hey cowboy, let's dance."

She started to drag me to the center of the dance floor. I glanced around, hoping to find anyone else before I got snagged into a dance with Lindsay. The new cowboy at the Kisment ranch, Grayson, leaned against the wall, watching couples dance. He was shy from what I could tell. He barely spoke two words to me the three weeks he's been working, but I heard the ladies thought he was pretty handsome. What a perfect opportunity.

"I've someone I want you to meet." I intertwined my fingers with hers and pulled her to the edge of the dance floor by the wall that Grayson was leaning against. "Have you met Grayson, yet?" Lindsay shook her head.

Grayson tipped his hat to her and said, "nice to meet you, ma'am."

She blushed and extended her hand towards his, "nice to meet you too."

"Would you like to dance?"

"Of course, I'd love to dance." She dragged him toward the dance floor. The poor cowboy didn't know what hit him. I smirked as I watched the two of them, retreating find Katie.

Katie

The wedding reception was in full swing. The band played, people danced, and I sat by myself in the corner. I swirled the contents of my glass around and looked into the depths. I'd heard rumors about Levi being a favorite of the ladies. I guess I never realized how much my heart wanted him, and it hurt when other girls flirted with him. I glanced up at that moment to see him with Lindsay, crossing the dance floor. They made a good pair with her long blonde hair and his with his black. I sipped my drink and scrolled through the photos from the wedding on my laptop.

A few minutes later, a shadow blocked out the light.

"Excuse me, ma'am. Can I Have This Dance?" His voice was low and husky.

My eyes slowly went up to his face. Levi's dark grey eyes are unreadable. He extended one hand to me.

"I'm not sure I can dance." I smiled tightly.

"It's easy. Just follow my lead, I won't even let you bump into people."

What should I do? My head said to refuse him even though it was rude. My heart begged, please just say yes.

"Please, Katie, can you dance with me?" The pleading and the sadness in his voice surprised me. He'd taken off his cowboy hat and was holding it in his hand, crushing the brim a little bit.

"Fine." I huffed.

I saved my project on my laptop and closed the lid. I set it next to the side by the pile of purses. Large hand engulfed mine as he helped me to my feet. He wrapped his arm around my waist, enfolding my right hand within his. He slowly spun me in a little circle to the beat of the music.

"Aren't we going to the dance floor?"

"Nah, it's too crowded." He spun me out and back in, holding me closer to his chest than he did before. My heart jumped to my throat as the butterflies twirled and skipped in my belly. It was becoming hard to breathe. The edges of my vision started to turn black. Levi stopped dancing and held me away from his body just a bit.

"Breathe, Katie," he whispered. "No need to have a panic attack. I just want to talk to you." His lips hovered inches from the top of my head but I heard him loud and clear. "Why don't we go outside?"

Night had fallen when he led me outside. We walked down the path and around the bend sitting by the fountain with the roses arching over it. He motioned me to sit down first. Then, he sat down next to me, our knees touching but our bodies angled away from each other. He held my hand in his and ran his thumbs up and down the skin of my hand. It was causing my heart to flutter. I'd never seen him so nervous. A little muscle ticked by his jaw as he chewed on his bottom lip. He's the one that wanted to talk I was going to wait him out.

"Here's the deal, Katie." He cleared his throat and swallowed a couple of times before going again. "I really like you."

With a jolt of surprise, I leaned over to meet his gaze, his gray eyes sucked me into their depths as I stared into his soul. "I like you too. I mean we've been friends forever."

"No, I like you more than friends. I like you and I want us to... maybe... no that's not right... I want us to go out."

I stared at him, dumbstruck. "But what about Lindsay and all the other girls."

"You're so cute." He tucked a long strand behind my ear. "There are no other girls. Lindsay's just flirting. She doesn't actually want to be with me."

"But what about your reputation as 'Love 'em 'n Leave 'em Levi.'"

"That's just all talk. I haven't dated anybody since high school. The only person that's ever owned my heart is you."

My heart pounded and blood rushed to my ears as he said those words. My hands shook and I swallowed a couple of times. "What?"

He grasped both of my hands, looking deep into my eyes. "I mean every word of it, Katie. You're the only woman I have ever thought of since I started working for your dad on the ranch. And you came out that summer, your beautiful blonde hair dyed black, wearing black eyeliner, and that black tank top. You thought that no one saw, that you were invisible to the world, but I saw you. You've had my heart ever since."

I stared at him. A tear rolled down from the corner of my eye. He caught it with his thumb and wiped it off.

"I don't know what to say."

"Say you'll be my girlfriend."

I nodded. He whooped, catching me into a hug. He lifted me and spun me around. Our lips collided and my butterflies did a happy dance. I slid down his front until my feet touched the ground. He cupped the back of my head as he angled over my mouth. I closed my eyes and kissed him back. Slowly, I came back to the present. I broke the kiss.

"What about when I go back to Denver?"

We pulled apart. He studied my face for a while. Tucking a lock of hair behind my ear, his hands slid up to frame my face.

"Let's date and do the long-distance thing. We'll figure it out. I've wanted to be with you for a long time. If I have to leave Texas, I will."

My heart burst with happiness. I squealed and launched myself at him. He caught me to his muscled chest. He slid a hand up to my cheek. The other one wrapped around my waist. Slowly, he brought his lips within inches of mine forward. Our lips touched. An explosion of fireworks set off between us. My mind went blank as I lost myself in the swirling and twirling of our lips. The kiss deepened and a groan escaped. It was perfect.

A voice clearing above us interrupted kiss.

"Are you two coming back to the dance or are you going to spend all night making out on the bench?" Kaleb's eyes smoldered as he smirked at us.

Blood flooded my cheeks. I tried to stammer out a response. Levi took off his hat, winking at me.

"We're going to spend all night kissing on this bench." He brought his hat in front of our faces as he kissed me again.

Epilogue

Six Months Later - Levi

I threw my last duffle bag into the back of my truck. I wiped the sweat from my brow and looked out over the Kisment ranch. The memories of my time on the ranch will always have a special place in my heart. Riding, working cows, and hanging out with my best friend. These were things that I'd never forget.

The tailgate slammed shut, bringing me back to the present. I turned to Kaleb as he leaned against the tailgate. His hat was pulled down to shade his eyes. Typical Kaleb, his expression was unreadable. He crossed his arms over his chest. A truck rumbled down the drive, flinging dust into the air. It slid to a stop next to mine. Pete climbed out of the cab with a wide grin on his face. His cowboy hat was pushed back his head.

"I didn't believe it when Kaleb told me this morning." He stuck his thumbs in his belt loops and rocked back on his heels. "I had to see for myself."

I laughed. "It's true. I'm moving to Colorado to be with Katie."

Pete reached into his back pocket and pulled out a large envelope. He handed it to me. It was stuffed full of money.

"What's this for?" I waved it at him.

"A bunch of us got together to chip in for your going away gift." Kaleb looked down at his boots. "The ranch doesn't pay well and...you might need it to get off your feet."

I looked at two of my closest friends. How thoughtful. "Thanks." I gave them each a hug. "It means a lot." I choked up.

"You'll always be welcome here unless you hurt my baby sister." Kaleb lightly punched me on the arm before heading into the barn.

"Maybe, when you come back, I could use a ranch foreman." Pete headed to his truck. "Drive safe."

"I'll come home for your wedding," I called at him.

Pete laughed. "You might be waiting a while." His truck started with a rumble and turned down the drive.

Shaking my head, I drove my truck down the drive and out of Texas to begin my new life with my soul mate. The lightness in my heart carried me to Colorado.

If you want to find out how Katie and Levi are doing in the future, head over to Alliebock.substack.com to get an extra epilogue!

If you enjoyed this story, please leave a review on your retailer/platform of choice! Thank you.

Falling for My Cowboy Chapter 1

Melanie

The sign said twenty miles to Sunnydale, TX and the nearest gas station. As I glanced down at my fuel gauge, the empty light flashed at me. Like I didn't know my car was starving; we were all starving! The last stop was over a hundred miles back, and I forgot to buy food. My stomach growled at me the minute I thought about all the things I didn't buy. I rubbed my abdomen in a circular motion trying to ease the hunger pains.

"Well, Benny, I hope we can make it."

I glanced over at my Beagle and rubbed his long brown ears. He was the best co-pilot a girl could ask for as he never complained about my driving or my choice in music. Benny opened his one good eye, giving me a long look before he yawned and went back to sleep. He didn't have a care in the world.

"I wish I had your life," I muttered to him before turning back to the stretch of highway.

The empty light stopped flashing as my car started to spit and sputter.

"No! No! Come on! We only have a few more miles to go."

With a last sigh, the car died as I guided it over to the shoulder of the road. I pounded my hands on the steering wheel in frustration, silently seething inside. I pulled out my cell phone, but all it said was "Searching for Service".

A tightness started in my chest and tears filled my eyes. *Come on, Melanie, hold yourself together.* The tears leaked out, running hot trails down my cheeks. Not this too, on top of everything. My retreat to my best friend stymied by a lack of fuel in my gas tank. *Just perfect. What to do now?* I looked over at Benny. He curled into a little brown ball, squeezing his one eye shut, totally ignoring me.

"Well, buddy, I guess we are going to have to hoof it to town." I wiped at my tears and blotted my mascara. "No need to have racoon eyes as we walk into Sunnydale" I muttered to myself.

I strained for his leash and my purse, both of which had slid under the seat. Next, I searched for some sneakers, or boots, or anything besides my cute strappy sandals. But, alas, in my haste to leave I'd only packed those super cute sandals and a couple of pairs of heels. *What was I thinking! Stupid, Melanie. Just stupid.* I grabbed the sandals without a heel, blew my bangs out of my eyes, and clipped on Benny's leash to start my trek into town. *I sure hope Sunnydale is more than just a one-horse town.*

The sweltering heat plowed into me when I stepped out of the car and onto the road: immediately, the sweat beaded on my back and ran down my body.

"Why is it so hot in South Texas? It's not even noon." I complained to Benny.

Of course, he didn't care. He was too busy sniffing all around, making happy little noises in his throat the way Beagles do as he explored the large cacti, flowers, and jackrabbit trails. The sun continued to beat down as we walked. Thirty minutes later, my shoulders were burnt and the dirt clung between my toes while I dabbed the sweat from my eyes. *How did everything fall apart? Where was my life going?* Sunnydale could not get here fast enough.

Pete

I was running late as usual. Nanna had a lot for me to do this morning, which put me behind schedule for an important meeting at the bank. I had to convince my loan officer, Mr. Dillard, to extend my line of credit. A headache formed between my eyes as I thought about how poorly the last meeting with him went. How could I keep myself afloat with all the loan payments I had? If I couldn't convince him, my life would change in a big way. Thankfully, Highway Four that ran from Nanna's place to Sunnydale was flat and straight. Country music blared from my speakers when I saw something up ahead on the shoulder. Sure enough, it was a car, a little red Honda with New York plates. I slowed my old Chevy truck as I approached. It appeared empty of people, but there were a lot of clothes in the back seat. "Interesting," I muttered to myself as I drove on to Sunnydale.

A couple of miles later, I came upon a woman walking a little dog on the side of the road. The truck slowed as I approached her from behind. Her tanned legs seemed to go on forever to end in the littlest pair of white shorts I had ever seen and she wore a spaghetti strap tank top that showed off beet red shoulders. She teetered on some pebbles, as her arms flailed, and she fell on to her white short clad bottom. I cringed, that had to hurt. I steered my truck up next to her and rolled down my window. *What kind of woman walked on the side of a highway in sandals and no sunscreen?* I had to find out.

"Excuse me, ma'am. Do you need a ride?" I leaned out the driver's side window.

She rose to her feet and pushed her shiny brown hair out her eyes to stare me down. Those eyes were so green I felt like I was looking into a pool; the swirling depths sucked me in. They were the prettiest eyes I had ever seen. Her brown hair reflected the sun at me. It looked soft as it floated around her shoulders; I had an urge to run my fingers through it. My heart constricted and missed a couple of beats. My mouth dried out and my tongue felt wooden as it sat heavy in my mouth. I swallowed a couple of times and rubbed at my chest. A throat clearing brought me back to the present. She straightened her clothes and pulled her shoulders back.

"How much farther to town?" An adorable Yankee accent tinged her words. She crossed her arms in front of her chest, pushing her breasts out even more. *Focus, Pete.*

"Hmm...about fifteen miles."

Her nose and forehead wrinkled as she threw out her arms. "Seriously? I thought for sure I was closer." *She was so cute.*

"No, ma'am. It's a ways, yet"

She shaded her eyes and glared down the road for a few minutes. "How do I know you won't abduct or murder me?" Her eyes snapped to me, demanding an immediate answer. *She sure was a feisty one.*

I smiled at her and winked. "You'll just have to trust me"

She pushed her bangs out of her eyes and picked up the Beagle. "Well, I'll just have to risk it. These sandals won't make fifteen more miles."

She pointed to her feet. The sandals in question were dusty and tattered. Red nail polish peeked through the dirt as she wiggled her toes. The truck door screeched open when she tugged on the door handle and her vanilla scent filled the cab when she hopped onto the bench seat. The Beagle jumped on to the middle seat and licked my face from ear to ear.

"Sorry, he's never met a stranger." She gathered him into her arms and held him tight. "He loves everyone."

The dog wiggled to get out of her embrace as she stared out the side window. Tension filled the cab as I drove to town. I flipped through a couple of stations and drummed my hands on the steering wheel, but those green eyes and shiny brown hair kept drawing my eyes to her.

"So, what's wrong with your car?" I broke the silence.

She jumped and turned towards me.

"Your car...you were walking," I offered her a blank look.

A blush crept up to her cheeks. *She really was cute.*

"I ran out of gas." She softly said and gazed down at her painted toes. She fell silent, again.

"Just trying to make conversation, but awkward silence it is," I muttered and looked back at the road.

"Sorry. It's just embarrassing to run out of gas"

"If you hadn't, I wouldn't be able to give you a ride." I flashed a smile at her. "It happens all the time. In fact, I ran out of gas last week."

"What did you do?" She turned her large green eyes toward me.

"I whistled and my horse came running in from the desert." I tried to keep my face impassive but she raised an eyebrow at me. "You know, like in the movies."

A snort escaped out of her nose. "Is that a joke?"

"Yep."

"It's not particularly funny." She returned to gaze out of the window.

We pulled into Sunnydale, past the veterinary clinic and cattle sale barn. Mike's Auto was on the corner of the only intersection with a blinking red light.

"I can drop you at Mike's. He owns the only gas station in town which also doubles as a fix-it shop."

She looked around the little town and turned those sea-green eyes back on me. "That will work." She gathered her Beagle and purse as I pulled into the bumpy yard of Mike's Auto. The gas pumps stood empty, the front windows were grimy, and the orange and yellow paint chipped on the Mike's Auto sign while the open sign blinked through a covering of dust.

"Thanks for the lift." Her lips thinned into a smile that didn't quite reach her pretty green eyes. "It was enlightening."

The dog leaped out of her arms and gave me lick that covered my face from chin to eyebrow and made me chuckle. I didn't have time to answer her before she slammed the truck door shut. *What a girl.* I shook my head to clear my thoughts as I climbed out after her. *Man, I was going to be late for my meeting with the bank.*

To read more of Pete and Melanie's story, go to alliebock.com!

Author's note

Analog photography has been making a quiet underground resurgence. There are still rolls of fim being sold and labs processing the film. Many of the hobbyists though do develop their film at home. They can have a simple darkroom that can be set up on the bathroom counter to extensive darkrooms. It was fun to research and dip my toe in the analog photography movement. I ended up enjoying it so much that I bought a Argus C3 and rolls of black and white film. Now to take some pictures!

If you enjoyed this story, please leave a review and share with your friends.

Acknowledgements

Writing a book has been a journey. It took a lot of time and patience, and I couldn't have done it without the help of a few people.

Thank you to my husband for being supportive of my writing, encouraging me to work on it even when I didn't want to, doing house chores, and being my first reader.

Thank you to Zack for being the one to question everything that happens in my stories.

Thank you to Jenna Kattric for reading the rough drafts, being supportive, and giving me the feedback that I needed.

Also by Allie Bock

Cowboys of Sunnydale
My Cowboy Crush
Falling For My Cowboy
Second Chance with My Bull Rider
My Unexpected Hero
My Cowboy of Convenience

Watch for more at www.alliebock.com.

About the Author

After living all over the country, Allie resides in Minnesota where she spends the daylight hours working as an equine veterinarian. In the evening, she escapes to imaginary Sunnydale, Texas. She loves to write about strong heroines who overcome challenges to fall in love with handsome cowboys.

Follow her on Substack at alliebock.substack.com or visit her website at alliebock.com.

When she is not working or writing, she can be found reading and spending time with the love of her life and their Dachshund. When they aren't in the house, they are working cows or riding their horses across open fields.

Read more at www.alliebock.com.

www.ingramcontent.com/pod-product-compliance
Lightning Source LLC
LaVergne TN
LVHW091735300125
802574LV00002B/301